Great-aunt Ida and Her Great Dane, Doc

Illustrated by S. D. Schindler

# Great-aunt Ida

A Doubleday Book for Young Readers

By Leah Komaiko

# and Her Great Dane, Doc

14.95

A Doubleday Book for Young Readers
Published by
Delacorte Press
Bantam Doubleday Dell Publishing Group, Inc.
1540 Broadway
New York, New York 10036
Doubleday and the portrayal of an anchor with a dolphin are trademarks of
Bantam Doubleday Dell Publishing Group, Inc.
Text copyright © 1994 by Leah Komaiko
Illustrations copyright © 1994 by S. D. Schindler

Library of Congress Cataloging in Publication Data
Komaiko, Leah.
Great-aunt Ida and Her Great Dane, Doc / by Leah Komaiko;
illustrated by S. D. Schindler.
p.    cm.    94B4006
Summary: Taking a walk with Great-aunt Ida and her Great Dane, Doc,
seems slow and boring to a small boy, until an emergency arises in which
Aunt Ida shows her true spirit.
ISBN 0-385-30682-2
[1. Great-aunts—Fiction.  2. Great Danes—Fiction.  3. Dogs—Fiction.
4. Walking—Fiction.  5. Stories in rhyme.]
I. Schindler, S. D., ill.  II. Title.
PZ8.3.K835Gr    1994
[E]—dc20    92-34196    CIP    AC

Manufactured in Italy
February 1994
10  9  8  7  6  5  4  3  2  1
NIL

For Bob Schwartz, the late Great Pearl, and
my forever Nettie Rice

—L.K.

Great-aunt Ida and her Great Dane, Doc,
Live alone together in the last house on the block.
Now today's my day to visit at exactly three o'clock.
I am a child—this is not how I should play!
And Doc is only four, he must feel the same way.

Great-aunt Ida and her Great Dane, Doc,
Come together to the doorway at the second that I knock.
And every time Aunt Ida sees me,
She says, "Goodness, what a shock!
Dollie Dearie,
Hokey Pokey,
How you've grown!"
And her finger shakes, as pointy as a bone.
But I wish she'd just leave Doc and me alone.

"Now Doc, you sit right here with Dearie,
And you have a little talk.
I'll go put my things together,
And we'll take our little walk."
Then Aunt Ida goes to get her cane and cape,
And Doc looks at me—today we will escape.

Great-aunt Ida and her Great Dane, Doc,
Take a half an hour to walk halfway down the block.
And each old lady Aunt Ida sees,
She stops to say hello,
And Doc stands there right beside her,
Very polite, very slow,
But there's one thing I can tell you
That I'm positive I know:
If Doc and me could have our own way
We'd get up and GO, MAN, GO!...

Run, Doc, run!

All the way up to the top of the mountain.
We'd rope cattle on the prairie,

Be the first ones in the fountain.
Then we'd race
To the place
Where the bleachers are packed.

The whole town's come to see
Doc's and my circus act!
Great-aunt Ida can't do this,
But it's not her fault.
You need courage to try
The deluxe somersault!
The real trick is to land up
On all of your feet…

But we're back with Aunt Ida,
Walking down the street.
And there's nothing to do here
But wait till we're done,
Until suddenly something says:
GET UP AND RUN!

A stray dog gang is coming—
They're out to have fun.

First they'll bite us to bits,
Every bone, one by one!

So Doc and I try
To start walking real fast,
But Aunt Ida says, "Slow down,
Let's make the day last."
She's just standing there smiling,
Can't she see that we're through?

Then she stretches—
And breathes deep and
Twists
And shouts,
"SHOOOOO!"

And they do!

Great-aunt Ida and her Great Dane, Doc,
And me
All walk together very proudly down the block.
Then Aunt Ida says,
"Time to go home.
It's almost five o'clock.
But will you give me one good-bye kiss on my cheek?"

Today I say, "Okay,
Can I come twice next week?"

### About the Author

**Leah Komaiko** is the author of many popular rhyming books, including *Annie Bananie, Aunt Elaine Does the Dance from Spain,* and *Broadway Banjo Bill.* This is her fourth book for Doubleday. Leah Komaiko lives in southern California, where she plans to stay, like Great-aunt Ida, forever young.

### About the Illustrator

**S. D. Schindler** has illustrated an impressive range of books, including Ursula K. Le Guin's two Catwings tales; *Children of Christmas* by Cynthia Rylant; and *Is This a House for a Hermit Crab?* by Megan McDonald, winner of the International Reading Association's Children's Book Award in the younger readers category. A naturalist as well as a painter, he lives with his family in Philadelphia.

### About the Book

The illustrations were created in gouache and watercolors. The book is set in 17-point Elan Medium. Typography by Lynn Braswell.